The *Rarest Puffball* in the *Universe*

Michael Pryor

Contents

One

Paradise for Alien Pets

Riley was on the way to change the water for the Martian sandworm when her floating display popped up and told her it was feeding time for the Jarken bat. Min was hurrying past with a basket of squeaky toys, and she grabbed his arm. "You want to help me feed the Jarken bat?"

Min frowned, took a banana out of his pocket and had a bite. "Jarken bat? Which one's that?"

"It's in B Block. It's shaped like a kite with little pointy ears, remember? From Milgon 4."

"Oh, *that* Jarken bat. Nice and colourful." Min stopped chewing his banana.

"Wait – what does it eat?" he asked. "Nothing Min-shaped, I hope."

"Jarken bats only eat Jarken flowers," Riley said. Since it was Min's first day helping her, she had to explain a lot to him. "But they eat lots of them, and they need six meals a day."

"That's a lot of Jarken flowers."

"And that's why Mum has gone to pick up our daily Jarken flower shipment from the spaceport."

Riley liked helping at Universal Pet Resort, her mother's business, even though it was a lot of work. She was glad her best friend Min had asked if he could come along, too. He was learning fast. He had to, really, because when you take care of alien pets there's a lot to learn. So many different aliens, so many different pets!

Riley had just turned twelve. She was determined to show her mother how responsible she was because her mother was working very hard to make Universal Pet Resort a success. And more responsibility would surely lead to a nice raise in Riley's pocket money! Anyway, how hard could it be? Almost all the systems were automated, there were plenty of robots to help out and everything was working nicely. Taking care of a few alien pets? No problem!

Universal Pet Resort was right next to the busiest spaceport on Earth. It got a lot of business from alien workers who needed to travel to other worlds and wanted a safe place to leave their pets while they were away.

The trouble with alien pets was that they needed special accommodation. Big alien pets needed accommodation that was spacious. Tiny alien pets needed snug accommodation. Crawling alien pets, flying alien pets, swimming alien pets and dangerous alien pets all needed their own special type of temporary home.

On top of that, they all had their own special requirements. They needed special food. They needed special liquids. They needed special sleeping quarters, lighting and habitats. Some of them even needed special atmospheres. So each area of the resort was really a unique facility of its own. Universal Pet Resort was a big, complicated business, and Riley loved it.

She loved all the different pets and all their different needs. She loved feeding them, exercising them and making sure they were well and happy. She loved the silky fur of the gossamer snakes from Loj. She loved the rough-and-tumble play of the sun hounds from Mellibean. She loved the silvery song of the tiny sheembles from Eskeroovian.

When she grew up, Riley wanted to be an alien zoologist and travel across the galaxy to see these creatures in their home worlds. Her dream was to visit strange new planets and explore polar ice caps, searing hot deserts and mountains so jagged they seemed to pierce the sky. She would observe rare animals in their natural habitats and learn about how they lived. The galaxy was full of life, and she wanted to see it all. But for now, rather than Riley going to the animals, the animals were coming to her.

At Universal Pet Resort Riley had seen how concerned customers could be when they left their pets in her mother's care. Part of her mother's job – and now Riley's as well – was to convince these clients that Universal Pet Resort was the safest, cleanest and most luxurious accommodation for their special buddy, whether it had wings, scales and enormous teeth or was a shapeless blob of jelly.

Two

Min the Curious

Any passenger on a spaceship landing at the spaceport could see that Universal Pet Resort was in the shape of a large semicircle with six interconnected buildings. At the centre was Main Block, which housed the customer service counter, the staffroom and Riley's mum's office. The other five buildings – A, B, C, D and E – radiated out from Main Block like the rays of a rising sun, each one connected to its neighbour by a corridor at the extreme end. Each block contained special enclosures for the pets.

In the large, leafy Jarken bat enclosure in B Block, a red and blue creature flitted from branch to branch. It came to rest above Riley and Min's head.

Riley settled her basket of Jarken flowers on the mossy ground, next to Min's.

"Easy now," she said softly to Min as she backed toward the gate. "Jarken bats hate loud noises. And whatever we do, we don't want to make a Jarken bat angry."

"I won't," Min said. "I'm Quiet Min, Min the Soothing, Min the Non-Threatening. See how serene I am?"

"I get it," Riley said. "I just hope the Jarken bat does, too."

"Why?"

"Because when Jarken bats get angry, they roll up into a ball and start to smell."

"Smell? Smell like what?"

"Believe me, you don't want to know."

"Hey, I'm Curious Min as well as Quiet Min. I have to know!"

Riley put her hands on her hips and lowered her voice. "Think of the worst, most horrible-smelling thing you know. Then imagine it gets buried underground for 100 years, then soaked in a vat of chemical waste for 100 years, and then left in a school bag for 100 years. That smell would be like a tiny whiff of angry Jarken bat."

Min bowed. “You know so much, oh wise one. Be kind and teach me.”

Riley threw a Jarken flower at him. It stuck to his ear.

After they had closed the sliding door behind them, the screen on the outside showed the Jarken bat diving toward the basket of flowers, which disappeared in a whirl of blue and red.

“It has a good appetite,” Min said, peering at the screen outside the enclosure.

“That’s an excellent sign,” Riley said. “When an animal won’t touch its food, it’s always time to worry.”

“Speaking of food,” Min said, “isn’t it lunchtime?”

“It’s only ten o’clock!”

“Snack time, then. I need another banana.”

They made their way past enclosures containing nollisterns, screeching gorx and a pair of blue xanthans, which were staring at each other with strange, almost human faces. Once outside B Block, they made their way to Main Block.

The staffroom was plain: two refrigerators, a sink, a table with mismatched chairs and a vending machine full of munchies. Min sat on a steel mesh chair and peeled another banana. He flipped through his floating display, humming happily and sharing little info nuggets with Riley.

"Hey," he said. "Did you know that three football teams on Milgon 4 have the Jarken bat as a mascot? And that seeing three Jarken bats together is supposed to be lucky?"

With all the possibilities of the Galaxy Wide Web, Min spent most of his online time watching the news and searching for interesting facts. Riley had never understood it. Instead of playing games or learning about celebrities, Min preferred keeping up to date with politics, current affairs and science stuff. It was strange, but Riley had decided it was a harmless habit that sometimes came in handy. Min knew what was going on, that was for sure. And if he didn't know, he was quick to find out.

Riley was poking about in one of the fridges when her floating display came to life in front of her eyes. She pushed the ghostly graphics and text to one side, but they sprang back. One block of text turned red and vibrated – an important message from her mum. *Riley! I'm stuck at the spaceport, and I've been notified that Ambassador Garfleplex is bringing in her pet! I'll try to get there in time, but you might need to handle the registration and admission.*

Three

The Ambassador Arrives

Riley smiled. Another chance to prove how responsible she was! Then she hesitated. “Min, who is Ambassador Garfleplex?”

“She’s a Haphnian,” Min said as he peeled another banana, “and the most important alien ever to visit Earth. She’s going to be the chief mediator in the peace negotiations to end the war between the Pontroonies and the Sillnesseepi.”

“Who exactly are the Pontroonies and the Sillnesseepi?”

Min took a bite of banana and chewed it for a while before answering. “They live on different sides of the planet Woohoo 2 and have been battling each other for 900 years non-stop.”

Whoa. That sort of aggression was seriously worrying. "And what's the war about? It can't just be that they don't like each other's looks."

Min shrugged. "No one can remember. It seems the war is now only a tradition, but neither side wants to be the first to back down."

Riley groaned. Stupidity wasn't just a human trait, then. "I don't suppose there's more than one Ambassador Garfleplex?"

"Nope. Why?"

"She's coming here with her pet."

Min's eyes widened. "When?"

Another alert jumped up on Riley's floating display, pulsing in shocking red. "Right now! Quick, to the front desk!"

Riley got to the counter just as Ambassador Garfleplex bent her towering frame to squeeze through the front door. Her swarm of tiny helpers tripped and darted around her six feet, waving their data pads and arguing with each other. One of them plucked a data pad from another and tossed it in the air, cackling.

Ambassador Garfleplex was a typical Haphnian. She looked like a giant purple praying mantis with six legs and wicked claws. She had jaws that could bite through steel. Her wings, though, were beautiful. They mostly stayed folded along her back, but when she extended them they swirled with translucent rainbow colours.

Her voice came from a translator box strapped to her chest. It creaked and croaked like an old tree in the wind. "Small human person!" she said to Riley. "You take care of pets most delightfully?"

Riley gulped. "We do, Your Excellency."

"Most good goodness! You will take optimal care of Raffles while I save the Pontroonies and the Sillnesseepi and bring enormous prestige to your planet for hosting such an event!"

Riley swallowed again. The ambassador was a little scary. It was the claws, mostly. "Universal Pet Resort always takes the best care of every pet that stays with us, Your Excellency. If you provide the information we need, we can take care of your pet."

Riley pulled a form from her floating display and gave it a gentle push. It coasted over to the ambassador, who bent and peered at it for a few seconds before flicking it over to her helpers, who fought over it.

Min was finishing his last mouthful of banana. He nudged Riley. "I'd love a helper swarm," he whispered.

Riley had hardly noticed the genetically engineered little creatures. They were about the size of an orange but shaped like a four-legged crab, and they scurried around the ambassador's clawed feet. They went around on all fours but could stand on two legs if they needed to. Helpers could be mischievous, but they were very useful. Only important people had them. They took care of all sorts of things, such as schedules, timetables, appointments and reminders, and they loved doing it. Their whole existence was centred on helping their patron, and if they were denied the chance to do it, they moped around in desolation.

The ambassador snapped her jaws together. "Forms!" she said. "All over the galaxy, forms everywhere! I snap my jaws at the being who invented forms!" She glared at the floating form her helpers were fighting over, each one desperate to fill it out. "My helpers will take care of the details."

The helper swarm erupted in a chorus of excited squeaks. They had a task to do! So happy!

Riley nodded. "As you wish, Your Excellency. Now, where is your pet?"

"Raffles is still at the spaceport," the ambassador said. "She will be delivered here, where you will make her comfortable and most happy." She pointed at one of her helpers. It quivered, then shot upwards onto the counter waving its tiny data pad, which quickly expanded to full size.

Riley reached out and dragged a note from the data pad to her floating display. "Will the spaceport authorities release Raffles into our care with this permission?"

"Permission? Authorities?" The ambassador flung up her claws. "Details! I shake my claws at the being who invented details!" She shook herself. "Everything is in order, small human person. Now, fetch Raffles and take care of her! And make sure she has her favourite toy for comfort!" The ambassador flicked a claw toward her helpers. One of them leapt onto it, ran up her arm and whispered into the ambassador's ear canal. The ambassador nodded. "I will return here to collect Raffles in two of your months, small human person. Two months, not any other number of months! Two months only!"

"Of course, Your Excellency," Riley said. "Raffles will be ready and waiting for you."

With that, the ambassador eased back through the door with her swarm of helpers tumbling and squeaking in her wake.

"Wow," Riley said. "This is really important. No wonder my stomach is flipping and flopping."

"You're probably hungry," Min said. "Have a banana."

Four

VIP: Very Important Pet

The rest of the morning was extremely busy for Riley, and she was glad she had Min to help. Even though he didn't know much about the business, he was a quick learner.

When the spaceport authorities delivered the ambassador's pet, Min was able to use the automated systems to whisk the crate to the correct accommodation on a robo-trolley.

Riley had itchy fingers as she supervised Min. She desperately wanted to jump in as he slowly and carefully selected the options on the front counter display, but she knew he had to do it himself. If she took over, he would never learn. Still, she could offer advice.

The screen showed that the robo-trolley had taken the crate containing the ambassador's pet to the correct accommodation in B Block. "I usually select the 'Open Accommodation' option once the robo-trolley is in position," she suggested.

"I was just about to do that," Min said.

"Great. Good."

"Hey, you look nervous. Is anything wrong?"

"This is a very important pet, you know," Riley said. "We're responsible for it, and I want everything to be right when Mum gets back."

"I thought you were careful with every pet."

Min selected "Open Accommodation". The door slid up and the trolley rolled forward.

"We *are* careful with every pet," Riley said. "We're just being *extra* careful with this one."

The ambassador's helpers had insisted on Accommodation Type 22 Beta, which was a jungle environment. It was hot and steamy with lots of greenery and a good stretch of sand. As Min slid the control, the robo-trolley gently eased the crate onto the sandy floor. The door of the crate opened and a large pink fluffball squeezed out.

Riley couldn't help herself. "Aw, so cute! What a pile of puffy perfection!"

Min agreed. "Seriously, I want to smoosh that thing so much. Look how round it is!"

Raffles was the size of a beachball, very pink and very fluffy. It had no legs or tail or any other feature to disturb its long pink fur except for two round black eyes. When it rolled around, its eyes disappeared. They only appeared again when it stopped moving, blinking as if it had made itself dizzy. Did its eyes come back in the same place or a different place? Riley wasn't sure.

Min couldn't stop grinning. "What sort of animal is Raffles, exactly?"

Riley found the answer on the admission form. "Raffles is an Ollinber puffling."

Min pulled up some information on his floating display. "The Ollinber puffling is one of the rarest pets in the whole galaxy," he read. "Did you know that as well as being the friendliest beast in existence, it has no sense of smell? Probably because it doesn't have a nose, I guess."

"So cute," Riley repeated. She gathered herself. She was in charge now, and she had to be serious! It was hard, though, as Riley desperately wanted to hug that fuzzy pink wonder and squeeze its thistledown plumpness again and again.

Min nudged her. "You're making squeaky noises."

Riley shook herself. "I was just clearing my throat."

"The ambassador was clear that Raffles needs her special toy." Min's fingers danced over the crate's display. The crate tilted and a small rubber duck rolled out. It bumped into Raffles, who gave the most delightful squeak Riley had ever heard. Raffles spent a few minutes pushing the small rubber duck around and squeaking happily.

Riley's cheeks started to ache from smiling so much. "You can't get much cuter than that," she said.

Min nodded. "On a cuteness scale of one, which is a blobfish, to one hundred, which is the Aldebaran rainbow deer, I'd say Raffles is somewhere near a million."

"Agreed."

The robo-trolley picked up the transport crate and backed out. The door rolled shut. Reluctantly, Riley turned away from the sight of Raffles wobbling around her temporary home and pushing her favourite toy this way and that.

Riley felt proud. The rarest pet in the universe was a guest at Universal Pet Resort.

Five

The Trouble with Ulgans

Hours later, Riley's mum still hadn't come back with the supplies of fresh Jarken flowers. She had messaged, though. *Shipment held up in processing department. Could be here till dark!*

Extra responsibility, yay! Riley suggested some good e-books for her mother to read while she was waiting and got on with the business of keeping Universal Pet Resort running smoothly. Mostly that meant sending robots, or Min, to do the jobs Riley didn't want to do, while she wandered around inspecting the various pets staying in the facility. After all, an alien zoologist needed to be familiar with lots of different species, right?

After she had spent some time in E Block – the area accommodating aquatic pets in dozens of tanks, each with their own special type and temperature of water – Riley's display pinged. *Customer coming to front desk*, it announced.

The entrance to Universal Pet Resort monitored people approaching and calculated when they would arrive, to make sure the staff could get to the front desk before the customers. Riley ran, though, just to make sure. As she skidded behind the counter it took her a moment to recover her breath. Still, she was quicker than Min, who hurried in after her. He had thick rubber gloves on his hands, knee-length rubber boots, earmuffs and a face mask, and he was splattered from head to toe with mud.

"Looks like you had fun," Riley observed wryly.

Min stared at her for a moment before taking off his earmuffs. "When you told me to exercise the screeching gorx, you didn't tell me it liked to run around in a swamp. Is there any reason you forgot to mention that little detail?"

Riley grinned. "I thought you'd like a surprise."

"Good thing I checked the screen before I went in, otherwise I wouldn't have been prepared."

"Go and shower. I'll take care of the customers."

Min glanced at the display that showed the customers approaching. “Hey, they’re Ulgans.”

The two aliens entering Universal Pet Resort were very skinny, very tall and bright orange. They each had an extraordinarily long nose – like an elephant’s trunk – which waved about, sniffing the air. One had a fringe of blue feathers on top of its head, while the other’s feathers were green. They both wore black t-shirts with “Ulga Forever!” on them.

“Ulgans?” Riley queried.

“Well-known troublemakers with an excellent sense of smell,” Min said as he headed for the staffroom. “I reckon even Ambassador Garfleplex would find them hard work. Good luck!”

The two Ulgans approached the front desk. They had regular features, other than their noses, and their eyes were a beautiful shade of blue. They didn’t look like troublemakers.

“Greetings,” the taller of the two said. “We are official inspectors from the spaceport. We need to examine your facilities now.”

Riley frowned. Her mother hadn’t said anything about an inspection, and these two didn’t look like official inspectors. Those t-shirts!

"Is something wrong?" Riley asked.

"That is what we are here to find out," the lead Ulgan said, while the other glanced back toward the front door of the facility. "Immediate obedience is required."

Riley remembered one of her mother's rules. "I'm sorry. Can I see some identification, please?" she asked.

The lead Ulgan waved its trunk-like nose about. The other Ulgan wriggled its shoulders and then its nose.

"We are inspectors from the spaceport," the lead Ulgan repeated. "We need to inspect your facilities."

By now, Riley was very suspicious. "Not without ID, you won't."

The two Ulgans looked at each other again, wriggled and flapped their hands in a silent conversation, then tapped their trunks on their foreheads. The second Ulgan said to the first, very clearly, "I told you this was a bad idea."

The lead Ulgan turned back to Riley. "We left our identification in our room, on the bed ... or perhaps on the windowsill."

Riley crossed her arms on her chest. "Then you'd better go and get it."

The Ulgans came close to each other, put their foreheads together and flapped their hands, then stood up straight and hurried out of the front door, not looking back. Once they were outside, the second Ulgan gave the lead Ulgan a whack behind the ear.

Riley stared in amazement.

Min came back out, towelling his hair. "What did the Ulgans want?"

"I have no idea," Riley said. "But I have a feeling they'll be back."

Six

Not a Tourist Trap

Riley was eating her lunch at the front desk and flipping through puzzles on her floating display when the smart alarm went off.

She had been impressed when her mother bought the smart alarm and installed it. An artificial intelligence monitored the whole facility, and if anything was wrong, it activated the appropriate alarm. A minor problem like a clogged drain got a gentle beep and the details of the issue. A more serious problem caused a double beep. Medium-sized problems triggered an annoying bell that was very hard to ignore. Things scaled up after that to the ear-splitting sirens that warned of building collapse, meteor strike or tsunami.

The AI mustn't have thought this problem was serious because Riley's display gave an almost questioning *Boop?* as it showed the long corridor of B Block, overlaying it with the words "Unauthorised Presence".

Two figures were making their way along the corridor and scanning the entry pad of every enclosure.

"Hey," Min said over Riley's shoulder. He had a salad roll in one hand and a banana in his shirt pocket. "It's those Ulgans again."

Riley peered at the display. Even though the two aliens were wearing hats this time – strange conical headgear, one green and one blue – she was sure they were the same two Ulgans who had tried to get in earlier. They were wearing the same "Ulga Forever!" t-shirts for starters.

Riley bit her lip. She could contact her mother, but if her mother left the spaceport now, they might not have enough flowers to keep the Jarken bats happy. No, Riley would take care of it. After all, dealing with alarms was part of being responsible.

"Those troublemakers aren't going to make trouble in Universal Pet Resort," she said to Min. "Come on."

Riley ran toward the entrance to B Block. Min hurried alongside her. "I've been looking up stuff about the Ulgans," he panted. "They're troublemakers all right, but they're a bit of a joke, really."

"I'm not laughing," Riley said. She hit the entry pad, and the door to B Block scooted back.

"In their culture they gain fame by disrupting things."

"They sound like troublemakers to me."

"That's the idea, but they're actually not very good at it. When they try for a big win, a giant disruption, their plan usually falls apart."

"And that's a problem?" Riley asked.

"It is, because by messing up their own plans they sometimes mess up other species' plans. Ever heard about the Great Vinegar Flood of Ceti Alpha VI?"

"Nope." Riley peered through the doorway. Nothing. The Ulgans must be right up the other end.

"Ulgans planned to disrupt a trade negotiation between Denebians and Andorrians by turning off the lights in the conference venue, but they went to the vinegar factory next door by mistake. One of them tripped, hit a valve and released all the vinegar in the factory. It caused a huge wave that made the whole town smell for weeks."

"Did they disrupt the trade negotiations?"

"I guess so. Just not in the way they meant to. It seriously backfired on the Ulgans, though. They suffered the most from the vinegar smell because of their sensitive noses."

There they were! "Can I help you?" Riley called down the corridor.

One of the Ulgans was examining the keypad and screen of a room Riley knew was empty. The other whirled around and nearly tripped over its own feet.

"Sorry!" the Ulgan wearing the blue hat cried. "We are tourists who are very lost!"

Green Hat flapped its hands. "We have never been here before, and we have never been spaceport inspectors either!"

Riley marched toward them, making sure she had her stern face on. Min trotted beside her. "How did you get here?" Riley demanded. "You didn't come through the front entrance."

The Ulgans looked at each other for a moment. Blue Hat addressed Riley. "We wanted to see the sights, for we are tourists. I accidentally tripped and stumbled through that door back there."

The Ulgan pointed along the corridor. Right at the end was the emergency exit door. Riley frowned.

It could have been left open by accident. Maybe.

"You take the big one," Min whispered to Riley. "I'll tackle the little one. Then we can find out what they're up to."

"Stop it," Riley whispered back.

"Go back that way," she ordered the Ulgans. "This is a respectable business, not a tourist trap."

Green Hat blinked. "No sights to see? We should leave immediately."

"That's right," Min growled, waving a half-eaten banana at them. "No trespassing, no breaking in and definitely no troublemaking."

The Ulgans scurried off and went out through the emergency exit door. Riley checked to make sure the door was firmly shut this time.

"And what do you think they're up to?" Min asked, taking a bite of his banana.

"I have no idea," Riley said. "But I don't think it's anything good."

Seven

Double Trouble

Busy, busy, busy. There was so much to do at Universal Pet Resort! Riley was starting to understand why her mother was so tired all the time. Some of the pets needed exercising on their robotic exercise machines. Others needed food at odd times, and some of that food was very, very strange.

Riley was glad she had Min with her. He was pretty cheerful about it all, and he kept rolling out interesting bits of information.

"Did you know that sun hounds can't look behind themselves?" he asked her as they adjusted the light levels in the accommodation housing the sleek animals. "Something to do with their neck bones."

"Really?" Riley said. She'd found this was a good, all-purpose response to Min's info nuggets.

"And their second pair of ears can hear colours."

"Really?" Riley frowned. According to her floating display, the light was still too dim for the sun hounds. She might need to call a repair crew.

"And how about this? Sun hounds can sleep for more than twenty-two hours a day."

"That'll have to do," Riley said as she shifted the illumination to maximum. She still wasn't happy, though. "Do we have the contact details for a good light-repair crew?"

Min busied himself with his display. "When do you want to get them here?"

"As soon as possible."

Ten minutes later, Riley was impressed when two repair robots whirred up to the front desk. They were tall, with many extendible arms, and hovered smoothly a few centimetres above the floor. "Many Hands Light Repairs," one of them said in a mechanical voice. "You have a light problem?"

"The illumination in Accommodation 14 in D Block seems to be malfunctioning," Riley said.

"We will fix it straight away," the other robot said. "After all, Many Hands make light work."

Riley stared. *Did that robot just make a joke?*

She flicked the directions to them from her floating display and opened the sliding door to D Block. The robots glided off as Min came back from A Block, wiping his hands on a wet cloth.

Riley's brow furrowed. "That's strange."

"What's strange?" Min crowded close to see the desk display.

"Those repair robots haven't gone to the right place."

"Are they lost?"

"They shouldn't be. I gave them the right location coordinates."

"Where are they now?"

"They're in B Block."

"That's where Raffles is!"

Riley pointed at the screen. "Look!"

The two robots had rolled up in front of Raffles' accommodation. Riley and Min watched in shock as both robots shuddered, then split, and two familiar figures climbed out.

"The Ulgans!" Min yelped. "They were operating those fake robot shells from inside!"

Riley frowned, thinking. "You said that Ulgans win respect by being troublemakers."

"That's right. The more trouble and disruption they cause, the more admiration they get."

"What if an Ulgan disrupted important peace negotiations between two species that have been at war for 900 years? How much credit would they get?"

It took Min a while before he could reply. "If they could do that, they'd be worldwide celebrities on Ulga. They'd be so famous that everyone would know their names. Their faces would be on t-shirts. A movie would probably be made about their exploits!"

"And would stealing the precious pet of the most important person in the peace negotiations, making her horribly upset and unable to go ahead with the job of bringing the Pontroonies and the Sillnesseepi together, be a good way of disrupting proceedings?"

Min's eyes got even wider. "It'd be such a clever plan that all Ulga would stand and applaud." He had to steady himself against the counter. "These Ulgans are going to steal Raffles, aren't they?"

Riley straightened, adjusting her Universal Pet Resort top. "Not on my watch." She put a hand on Min's shoulder. "We've never had a pet stolen from Universal Pet Resort, and it's not going to happen today."

The Ulgans had left their fake robot shells at the top of the corridor. Riley peered past them. The door to Raffles' accommodation was open.

"We should call the spaceport police," Min whispered.

"Yes, good idea," Riley whispered back. "But we can't wait. We have to do something now, or they'll get away."

An Ulgan poked its head out of the doorway and looked up and down the corridor. Riley and Min pulled back in a hurry.

"What are we going to do?" Min asked. "They'll be out of here in minutes!"

"I have an idea." Riley pulled up her display. "The Jarken bat's accommodation is opposite the one Raffles is in," she said. "And I was thinking of making it a little bit angry."

"You want the Jarken bat to smell bad?"

"I want the Ulgans and their sensitive noses to experience the worst smell in the galaxy."

"How do we make the Jarken bat angry enough to let loose its smell?"

"How about I get the smart alarm to do something dramatic?" Riley proposed.

Min grinned. "We'd better put on earmuffs first."

Eight

The Jarken Bat's Revenge

An ear-splitting siren went off in the Jarken bat accommodation. Even though the door was closed, the din echoed up and down the corridor like a herd of Rigellian screamers with very bad headaches.

This was no ordinary siren; it was the smart alarm's top setting, and it had never been used at Universal Pet Resort. It was meant to be kept for major emergencies, such as the appearance of a 5-kilometre-tall monster who just wanted to stomp on buildings. When Riley opened the Jarken bat's door, she could still hear the sound through her earmuffs because it was loud enough to bore through concrete. It also had a horrible up-and-down tone that set her teeth on edge.

Min was holding his stomach. That noise was horrible! Riley started to feel sick, too, and her eyes were watering.

After a few seconds of this torture, she had to turn off the siren. She couldn't stand it.

"Thanks," said Min as he took off his earmuffs. "My ears are ringing."

Riley took hers off, too. "So are mine."

Riley peered down the corridor. What about the plan? Was the Jarken bat angry?

Min yelped. He grabbed his nose and flapped his other hand in front of his face. "What a stink! And we're 50 metres away! I'd hate to be up close!"

Riley squeezed her nose tightly. Her watering eyes started to sting. "By all the constellations in all the galaxies across the entire universe, that's a horrible smell!"

"You weren't exaggerating," Min said in his squashed-nose voice. "It could make your nose bleed." He shook his head. "I think I need to go and have a lie down."

Riley grabbed his arm. "Not yet. Look."

One of the Ulgans appeared, clutching at the doorway of Raffles' accommodation. It was hunched over, with its head hanging low, as it staggered into the corridor. Its trunk-like nose was flailing about as if the nose was trying to escape all on its own.

The Ulgan leant against the wall and slid slowly down until it was sitting on the floor. Its trunk waved feebly, and it groaned.

The other Ulgan wobbled out of the accommodation, tripped and stumbled for a few metres before curling up on the floor next to its partner.

Riley and Min hurried over, rolled both the Ulgans into an empty enclosure next door and shut them inside.

A cute pink fluffball poked out of the doorway behind them. "Raffles!" Riley called.

"That's 100 per cent adorable alien," Min said.

"Now I understand why the ambassador likes Raffles so much," Riley breathed. "Have you ever seen anything cuter?"

"Never." Min smiled. "I've turned on the air-cleansing system. When that smell's gone, and after we've called the police, I think we'd better come back and check Raffles is really okay, don't you? Just in case."

Nine

A Noble Peace Surprise

When the spaceport police arrived, Riley and Min explained what had happened. The officer in charge couldn't stop smiling. "We've been after these two pests for a long time," she said as her team took the queasy Ulgans away. "We'll make sure they don't make any more trouble for a long, long time."

After that, Riley and Min returned to the front counter. Riley had to supervise the cleaning robots in a super-deep clean of B Block to get rid of the Jarken bat smell. Even with the air-cleansing system and as many doors open as possible, it was a tough job. The smell was so bad it even made the entire Universal Pet Resort computer system hiccup a few times, which made Riley nervous.

Riley watched on her display as the cleaning robots blasted the corridor walls and ceiling with warm soapy water, scouring the ceramic surface clean. Min worked alongside her, moving the B Block pets to other quarters so their accommodation could be made stink-free. He had to organise the robots that put the pets in their special transport crates and then find room for them in the other blocks. It was like moving chess pieces around on a board, and Min loved it.

"Guess what?" he asked Riley as he worked away. "I've just found out that Raffles is such a rare beast that nobody really knows much about her at all. The Galactic University desperately wants to study her because there are rumours she can change her shape."

"Shapeshifting? Really?" Riley made adjustments so that the cleaning robots went to work with whirring brushes. They made the tiles sparkle. It was slow but important work. No more Jarken bat smell!

"And she's so squooshy they think she can even triple her size or shrink herself down to the size of an orange."

"Amazing. I can see why the Galactic University wants to study her."

“Yep, but Ambassador Garfleplex won’t let them touch her best buddy. Raffles is too precious.”

Riley nodded absently. She was concentrating on the final stages of the cleaning program. Now that the cleaning robots had their orders, they should be able to continue the work by themselves. Riley would check now and then, just to make sure, of course. It was the responsible thing to do.

“Uh-oh,” Min said.

Riley turned to him. “I don’t like the sound of that ‘uh-oh’. What’s up?”

“You know how the war between the Pontroonies and the Sillnesseepi has been going for 900 years?”

“You told me that.”

“And you know how it was going to be impossible for Ambassador Garfleplex to get to them to sign a peace treaty?”

“She didn’t think so. She said it’d take months, but she was confident she’d get it done.”

“Well, she was right about getting it done. They came to an agreement. In less than a day, Ambassador Garfleplex has put an end to a 900-year-old war! She’s a hero,” said Min. “They’re having huge celebrations over at the conference centre.”

"Oh, wow!" Riley said.

"Everyone said it was impossible," Min said. "The Pontroonies and the Sillnesseepi are sworn enemies and can't stand the sight of each other."

"A 900-year war, and Ambassador Garfleplex managed to put an end to it, just like that."

"And she's done it in a few hours – amazing!"

"Amazing, all right. But that means –"

Riley didn't get to finish. Her floating display had been dormant while she was concentrating on the cleaning, but now it sprang up in front of her eyes. A text block vibrated. *Warning: important customer approaching*, it read.

"Ambassador Garfleplex is here. She must have left the celebrations early," said Min.

Riley grabbed Min by the shoulders. "You've been reorganising the pets. Where did you put Raffles?"

"Hold on a second," Min said. He pawed through the data on his floating display. "And a second more." He flipped data to one side and then the other. "Nearly there." He started to look sick, and Riley had a very bad feeling. "You know what?" Min opened and closed his mouth a few times before he found the right words. "I think we've lost Raffles."

Ten

The Problem with Puffballs

Riley's stomach was doing flip-flops when Ambassador Garfleplex marched in with her helper swarm. "Where is my Raffles?" the ambassador demanded. "I want my Raffles!"

"Ah, Your Excellency, congratulations." Riley said. "You were successful! What a triumph!" She snatched a glance at Min. He was frantically scrabbling through the counter's floating display and trying to find where he'd put Raffles. His hands snatched and rearranged the data in front of him as he searched, shaking his head and trembling a little. Ambassador Garfleplex was a truly scary sight.

The ambassador stomped from one side of the customer service area to the other. Then she stomped to the door, where she whirled, causing her helpers to tumble over each other, squeaking. "Where is my Raffles?" she boomed.

"I'm sorry," Riley said. "We weren't expecting you, as you've arrived early."

"Early? I am never early! The time I arrive is the right time, whenever it is!" Ambassador Garfleplex straightened herself. As she was already so tall, this meant she nearly bumped her head on the ceiling. Her helpers scurried around her, hopping from foot to foot to foot to foot, squeaking and trying to catch her attention.

One of the helpers was waving a screen. The ambassador clicked her wings together and lowered her long neck so she could peer at the screen. She rattled her wings together rapidly, and Riley swallowed. It sounded far too much like weapon fire.

"Harrumph," Ambassador Garfleplex said. "So I am early. It doesn't matter. What matters is I am here! Where is Raffles, small human person?"

Min hissed as he pushed a data block over to Riley. "I'm sorry," Riley said to the ambassador. "Our records say that you were due to pick up your pet in two months time. We're not ready right now."

The ambassador waved a claw. "This month, next month, three months – no difference! I want Raffles now!"

One of the helpers broke away from the swarm and leapt up onto the counter. It scurried over and held up its data pad to Riley. *The ambassador is angry*, it read.

"No kidding," Riley muttered.

The helper wobbled a little, flipped the data pad around, went to work on it, then turned it around again. *The last time the ambassador was angry in a shop, two retail assistants were eaten.*

The helper didn't wait for Riley's reaction. It whirled around, leapt off the counter and rejoined the swarm.

Riley looked at Min. Min looked at Riley. They both swallowed at the same time.

Riley waited until she was sure she could speak without her voice trembling. "I understand you are anxious to have your pet returned to you, Your Excellency."

"Raffles! I must have Raffles!" The ambassador snapped her front claws together.

Min slid another text block over to Riley, who tried to remain calm as she said, "Ah, I'm sorry,

Your Excellency. Can you excuse me for a moment? I need to discuss something with my colleague."

"Raffles!" the ambassador croaked. "Raffles will be missing me! She will be sad and blue! Miserable Raffles, Lonely Raffles, Raffles the Disconsolate!"

"Not for much longer," promised Riley. She grabbed Min by the arm and dragged him into the staffroom behind the counter.

Riley closed the door carefully and turned to Min, who was shifting from one foot to the other. "What do you mean we've lost the ambassador's pet?"

"Hey, don't yell at me. I didn't lose Raffles. The system did. When I was shifting pets out of B Block for the clean-up, there was a glitch."

"You didn't tell me about a glitch."

Min shrugged. "The system hiccupped a couple of times."

Riley gasped. "The Jarken bat smell! While I was cleaning, I think it affected the system."

Min nodded. "I wouldn't be surprised. A hiccup, a glitch and a few pets got jumbled up and went into the wrong accommodation. It was like musical chairs, really, and I thought I had it sorted out."

"So where's Raffles? Can't we scan everywhere until we see her? She's hard to miss, that bright-pink fluffball."

"I tried. No sign."

"How can that be?"

"Remember the shapeshifting? Raffles could look like anything now!"

Riley closed her eyes. This was a disaster. Even if she didn't get eaten by Ambassador Garfleplex, her mother would hear she'd lost an important pet.

This wasn't being responsible. Riley was letting her mother down.

Eleven

The Great Escape

Min tugged on Riley's arm. "Look, the transport crate is still in Raffles' original accommodation. Bring it to the front counter, and in the meantime I'll work out a way to scan for something that used to be a giant pink pom-pom."

Riley and Min went back to the counter. Ambassador Garfleplex was stalking up and down, attended by her helper swarm. When Riley reappeared, the ambassador rattled up to the counter. "You have Raffles?"

"Not yet, Your Excellency. We can't hurry these things. Every pet at Universal Pet Resort gets the best, most careful care, especially when leaving," Riley assured her.

The ambassador looked puzzled. Riley quickly added, "We need to give them a complete check-up and undertake a thorough cleaning routine for freshness and joy."

"Nice one," whispered Min, who was standing at her side and feverishly flying through data, searching for Raffles.

"Ach!" The ambassador tilted her head back, clashed her claws together and shook them at the ceiling, but then she reconsidered. "No, this is good. Raffles can be delicate. Take care, small humans, and deliver Raffles to me in good health!"

Riley spoke up bravely. "We return all pets to their owners in tip-top condition, Your Excellency. Now, you can come back in a few hours, or you can wait here."

The ambassador waved her claws. "Hours?"

A helper ran up the ambassador's leg onto her body and then to her shoulder. It squeaked into her ear canal. The ambassador nodded. "Hours are units of human time. I have time. I will wait here until my Raffles is brought to me!"

Four or five helpers huddled and then broke away from the swarm. They bustled towards the counter and climbed over each other to reach the top. They fought and squawked to present a data pad to Riley. *The ambassador thanks you for your service. She will not eat you as long as Raffles is returned in perfect condition*, it read.

Riley smiled and nodded, pretending that everything was fine and under control. It was the most difficult smile she'd ever smiled, but she managed it.

The helpers on the counter tumbled over each other, darting in all directions. One of them ran around and rudely peered at Riley's floating display, before jumping up and kicking the data so that it broke apart and reassembled into nonsense. The helper cackled, then scuttled over and lunged at the banana in Min's pocket. Min squawked just like a helper as he swatted it away.

The naughty helper tripped and stumbled its way back to join the other helpers, who were teeming around Ambassador Garfleplex's feet.

The ambassador snapped her claws together, positioned herself in the corner of the customer service area and watched Riley with her huge glittering eyes.

The helpers circled around the ambassador for a while until they clustered at her feet.

Min scratched his cheek. "I really could use a helper swarm."

Riley hardly heard him. She was staring at her floating display. "Min, when you were trying to find Raffles, did you hit the 'Release All' command?"

Min looked puzzled. "I didn't know there was a 'Release All' command."

"It's for emergencies," Riley said slowly. "Like an earthquake or a black hole wandering by."

"Uh-uh, not me. Not even in my most absent-minded daydream would I hit a 'Release All' command." Min's eyes were wide. "Are you saying all the pets are out of their accommodation units?"

"That helper who kicked my data around," Riley said softly. "It must have accidentally disturbed the system."

In the distance, Riley could hear ominous hooting and wailing. "Min, you know how I said we were in trouble?" she asked.

"Yes."

"I want you to double it and double it again."

Twelve

Pet Wrangling

Riley's fingers blurred as she quickly hit the "Close All" command.

"The doors weren't open long, but some of the pets are loose. They've been wandering up and down the corridors and into each other's enclosures!" she exclaimed.

"What if Raffles is one of the escapees?" Min asked. He was jumping from foot to foot.

"Then finding her has just become even harder."

Riley opened the robot system on her floating display and ordered all the mechanical assistants to get out there and herd the pets back into their proper accommodation units. She shook her head.

"We don't have enough robot assistants."

Min put up his hand. "I volunteer to pop over to Robots R Us and buy a dozen state-of-the-art robots. I won't be more than an hour or two."

"There's no time for that, Min!"

Min shrugged. "It was worth a try."

"The robot assistants we have can take care of four of the five blocks, but that means there's one left over."

"I bet there's only one thing to do, right?"

"Right. We have to get out there and do what needs to be done. Follow me."

Riley sprinted into the office. Inside, she unlocked the big grey cabinet and grabbed a net shooter, a pair of heavy-duty gloves, a dart belt and a broom. Min stood in the doorway and stared. "What's all that for?"

"I want to be prepared for anything." Riley checked there were darts in the belt and strapped it on. "You'd better be, too."

"Eep!"

While she waited for Min to buckle up, Riley called up her floating display and zipped through all the monitoring cameras. She groaned. Scene after scene showed pets bumbling around where they shouldn't be. An Iskian flubberwing was wrestling with a Womersley lug. It looked like friendly play, but it was hard to tell with the flubberwing's feathers flying around like that. A Yuthian slinker was crawling along the ceiling in A Block. Was it stalking that Vallidian glass cat? If it was, it was going to get a nasty surprise.

"Ready!"

Riley whirled around. Min had a belt full of tranquiliser darts strapped across his chest. He had a scanner helmet, two dart guns and a rope spinner, and his gloves sparked when he clapped them together. "Whoops," he said.

Riley pointed. "Grab a mop."

"What for? I've got all this hi-tech pet-wrangling gear!"

"Pets on the loose means plenty of cleaning up!"

Riley ran for B Block first, because even though Universal Pet Resort was in uproar, the most important thing was finding Raffles.

Riley and Min stepped through the double doors and into a riot. A scaled beast as big as a cow was using all six legs to waddle away from them. Something small and bird-like was perched on its broad, round back, burbling away happily.

Two snake-like creatures had become tangled and were rolling along like a hoop.

Dozens of other pets were hopping, flapping, galloping, springing or trudging up and down the long, narrow corridor between the open doors.

Min had both dart guns in his hands. "Yikes! Where do we start?"

"Look out!" Riley cried.

A brown, furry, flat shape dropped from the ceiling and landed in front of them. As it shook itself, it opened a mouth full of big, sharp teeth.

Riley stepped in front of Min to stop him shooting. She reached out a hand. The furry thing lolloped over and rubbed itself against Riley's hand.

"It's growling!" Min yelped.

"It's purring." Riley took her broom in both hands. "Open the door of Accommodation 1."

Min punched the keypad. Riley used the broom to steer the Ossian thalber inside. It dived into a pile of stones, purring happily.

"Right," Min said. "One down, plenty to go."

"Let's get to Raffles' original accommodation," Riley suggested. "If we're lucky, she'll still be in there."

"Looking like what, though?" Min asked. He ducked as a sparkly, star-shaped pet bounced up and off one wall, then another, and finally back in the direction of a Magian puffer.

Raffles' accommodation, of course, was right up the end of the hallway. As Riley and Min worked their way along the corridor, they herded pets back into their units where they could. Sometimes, though, the pets were too quick. "They think we're playing with them," Riley said as a whirling eel shot past them and wriggled around a furry, sleeping Hollyban snorter.

Inside Raffles' accommodation, the soft yellow light shone on a transport crate that was lying against a bush. The lush vegetation stirred in the programmed breeze. Raffles' small rubber duck was sitting all by itself in the middle of the sandy floor.

"Right," Riley said to Min. "We'll check this place from top to bottom. If we're lucky, Raffles is just hiding."

Thirteen

Raffles on the Run

Riley moved forward first. She wasn't very happy about this, because if Min got jumpy, he was likely to shoot her in the back with the dart gun. He'd apologise, but that wouldn't help at all.

She tried to look in all directions. "You see anything?" she asked Min.

"Lots of things, but nothing that looks like a puffball – or anything that looks like it used to be a puffball either, I think."

Riley picked up the rubber duck. Maybe Raffles would come to it. "Here, Raffles! Here, girl! I've got your favourite toy for you!"

Riley and Min waited, motionless, but Raffles didn't appear.

Min patted Riley on the arm. His gaze darted up to the tops of the small trees, over to the bunch of rocks in the corner, around at the bushes and shrubs and up to the soft, hazy pretend sky.

"It was a good idea and worth a try."

Riley was downcast. What were they going to do? She sighed and tucked the duck in her pocket.

"Let's go Raffles hunting."

They stuck together as they moved through the accommodation unit. After checking the vegetation, Min crept around to peer behind the boulders.

"Nothing," he reported, "except this."

Min held up another rubber duck, identical to the one Riley had stowed away. "Raffles must really like rubber ducks," she said as Min handed the second one to her. She put it in her other pocket.

"Ambassador Garfleplex said they're her favourite toy." Riley sighed. "Two ducks, no Raffles."

"So she got out, then," Min said, "and maybe shifted her shape?"

Riley stood at the door. The corridor was still a riot. "We'll have to sort through them all one by one, and the leftover one will be Raffles."

"Good plan," Min said. "Can I shoot any of them with darts?"

"No. And turn off those electro-gloves, too."

"Can I use the rope spinner instead?"

"If you read the directions first. It could be handy if the Magian puffer refuses to move."

"I never read directions. They get in the way of my natural skill."

It took hours, but finally Riley and Min had all the B Block pets back in their proper accommodation units. Riley had to get the last few in by herself, as Min had tangled himself up badly while using the rope spinner.

But Raffles was nowhere to be found.

"We have to tell the ambassador that we can't find Raffles right now," Riley said to Min.

"Really? Can't we stow away on a spaceship and hide somewhere at the edge of the galaxy instead?"

Riley ran her hands through her hair. "Look, Raffles couldn't have got out of the complex. She must be in one of the other blocks," she said. "It might take time, but we'll find her."

Min peeled a banana and took a bite. "And you think you can explain that to Ambassador Garfleplex and she'll be okay with it?"

"I have to try."

Fourteen

The Quack Up

Riley and Min stepped out of the office and into the customer service area. Ambassador Garfleplex whirled around, sending her helpers flying in all directions.

"Raffles! You have Raffles?" she bellowed, rattling her claws.

Riley sighed. "We need to talk about that."

The ambassador advanced on the counter, her claws now snapping. "Raffles!"

Riley and Min stepped back. Riley's stomach felt as if it was getting ready to go on holiday a long way away, but she spoke up gamely. "I'm sorry, Your Excellency, but we've had a problem."

"A problem with Raffles?"

The helpers climbed up and over the ambassador and onto the counter. They piled on top of each other, squawking with excitement as the ambassador towered over them, glaring at Riley and Min.

As Riley put her hands in her pockets to stop them trembling, she felt something there. She pulled it out and blinked at one of the small rubber ducks that belonged to Raffles. She felt in her other pocket and pulled out the second duck. She'd forgotten she had them.

She put them on the counter. "Here, Ambassador. These are yours."

Riley and Min watched with trepidation as the ambassador leant forward, picked up one of the rubber ducks and held it gently in her claw.

The rubber duck quivered. It shook. It wriggled. Then, with a joyous squeak, it expanded into a large pink fluffball with two blinking black eyes. It squeezed out of the ambassador's claw and bounced up and down in the ambassador's arms.

"Raffles has had a good sleep!" the ambassador announced. "See how happy she is!"

Riley and Min looked at each other. Riley couldn't believe it. They'd been looking for a missing pet that hadn't been missing at all. It had been in Riley's pocket!

Riley shook her head. *Alien pets: you never know what to expect with them.*

Riley pulled up her floating display. "Just a few final things, Your Excellency, and you can be on your way."

The ambassador was swaying from side to side, crooning as she hugged Raffles. "More details? My assistants will take care of that!"

When the forms were completed, the ambassador reached down and picked up one of her helpers. She handed it to Min. "This is for you, small human person."

"For me?" Min's eyes opened wide.

"My assistants tell me you need assistance. Well, here it is. I praise the being who invented helpers, and so will you."

Min held the helper in the palm of his hand. It chirped, then held up its data pad, which enlarged to human size as Min peered at it.

"What's it saying?" Riley asked.

"It says it wants a bite of my banana."